# ANIMAL LORE & LEGEND

# OWL

American Indian Legends Retold by Vee Browne
Additional Text & Book Design by Vic Warren
Illustrations by Diana Magnuson

SCHOLASTIC INC.
New York Toronto London Auckland Sydney

The tradition of American Indian storytelling is older than history. Stories of the animals of North America have, for thousands of years, taught youngsters to honor and respect all forms of life. The authors are proud to bring this art form to the pages of this book, in the hope that we may entertain, educate, and inspire a new generation of children.

We are honored to retell these stories and wish to thank the Seneca, Zuni, and Picuris nations from which they come.

Additional thanks are due D. L. Birchfield for his technical assistance and the American Museum of Natural History Dept. of Library Services for the Salish grave post photo #31606 on page 13.

**Library of Congress Cataloging-in-Publication Data**

Browne, Vee.
    Animal lore & legend – owl / American Indian legends / retold by Vee Browne ; additional text & book design by Vic Warren ; illustrations by Diana Magnuson.
        p.    cm.
        Summary: Includes both factual information and Indian legends about North American owls.
    ISBN 0-590-22488-3
        1. Indians of North America – Folklore. 2. Owls –Folklore. 3. Owls – Juvenile literature. 4. Tales – North America. [1. Owls – Folklore. 2. Indians of North America – Folklore. 3. Owls.] I. Browne, Vee, 1956-  . II. Warren, Vic, 1943-  . III. Magnuson, Diana, ill., 1947-  . IV. Title: Animal lore & legend–owl.
    E98.F6A54 1995
    398.24'52897'08997–dc20                                    94-43935
                                                                                CIP
                                                                                AC

12 11 10 9 8 7 6 5 4 3 2 1          5 6 7 8 9/9 0/0

Printed in the U.S.A.                          09

First Scholastic printing, September 1995

Photos:
Title Page, Saw-whet Owls
Back Cover, Great Horned Owl

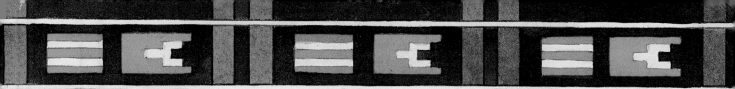

Vee Browne is a Navajo author and educator. She has written several children's books. She is a member of the Native Writers' Circle of the Americas and the Wordcraft Native Writers' Program. She has received the Buddy Bo Jack National Humanitarian Award for Children's Books. In 1992, she won the coveted National Cowboy Hall of Fame's Western Heritage Award for her book, *Monster Slayer*.

She lives in northeastern Arizona, in Chinle, on the Navajo reservation. The stories in this book have already been tested, and earned much applause from her own children, as well as from the kindergarten class she teaches.

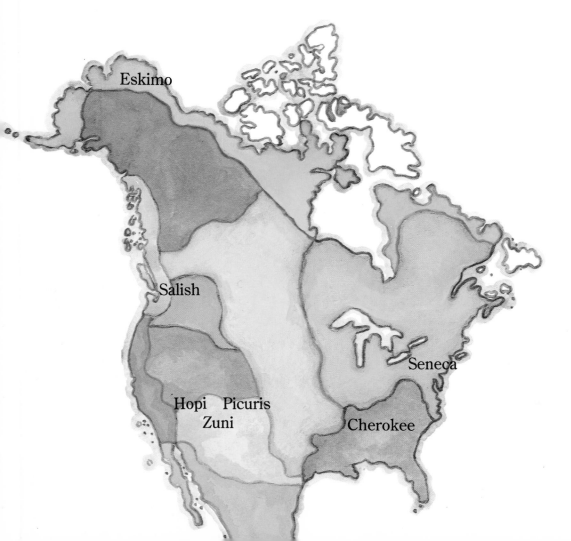

Barn Owl

Owls hunt at night.
They have large eyes.
They can see well in the dark.

Large owls hunt rabbits, squirrels,
skunks, rats, and snakes.
Small owls hunt mice, small birds,
and insects.

The biggest is the
Great Gray Owl.
It stands almost
three feet high.
Its wings spread
up to five feet.

There are 18
kinds of owls in
North America.

# OWL BIG EYES

A Seneca Story

This day, the Everything Maker,
Ra-wen-io, decided to make
animals and birds.

He walked through the deep,
deep forest.
He asked each fur coat and
feather coat how they wanted to be.

The big white owl, Oh-o-wah, sat in a
tree waiting his turn.
He flapped his wings and watched.

Ra-wen-io worked on Rabbit's ears.

Rabbit said, "I want nice long legs.
I want sharp fangs.
I want claws like Panther."

"Whoo-o . . . whoo-o," said Owl.

Ra-wen-io said, "Be quiet!
Turn your head.
Close your eyes.
No one shall watch me work!"

But Owl watched from his nest
on a branch.

"Whoo-o . . . whoo-o," hooted Owl.
"I want a nice long neck like Swan.
I want red feathers like Cardinal.
I want a long beak like Heron.
I want to be the best of all."

Ra-wen-io took Rabbit by the waist
and pulled his legs to make them long.
Owl rolled his eyes and blinked.
He turned his head to look.
Ra-wen-io saw Owl looking at him.

8

This was forbidden.
"I warned you not to look," he said.

"Whoo-o . . . whoo-o," hooted Owl.
"No one can tell me to not to watch."

This made Ra-wen-io angry.
He reached for Owl.
He pulled him down from the branch

He shook Owl. He pushed
his head down into his neck.
Owl's eyes grew big with fear.

Ra-wen-io pulled his ears until they
stuck up at both sides of his head.

"There!" said Ra-wen-io.
"That will teach you!
Now you have big ears to listen."

Ra-wen-io rubbed mud all over Owl.
Owl flapped his gray wings.

"Whoo-o . . . whoo-o," cried Owl.

"All Owls shall have short necks,"
said Ra-wen-io.
"You will never watch me again.
You will only be awake at night."
He put Owl into an old hollow tree.

Ra-wen-io went back to find Rabbit.
But Rabbit got scared and ran away.

To this day, rabbits are fearful.
And owls hunt them in the dark,
dark woods.

The Great Horned Owl lives in every Indian nation in North America.

Its horns are not horns or ears.
They are tufts of feathers.

Great Horned Owls live in old crow, hawk, or eagle nests.
Most owls live in holes in trees.
Some live in holes in cactus plants.

The Hopi say the Great Horned Owl helps their peaches grow.

Eskimo Owl Drawing

Owls have magic powers in many Indian stories.
The Cherokee name for the Great Horned Owl is *tskili*.
It means "magic maker."

Great Horned Owl

Salish Totem Pole

13

# THE PRAIRIE DOGS ASK OWL TO STOP THE RAIN

A Zuni Story

"Who will stop the rain?" asked the prairie dog chief.
"The Rain Gods keep dropping water. Our fields are flooded."

The hungry women and children in the wet holes all around cried,
"Wek  wek, wek wek, wek wek!"

They stood in the middle of a meadow. Nearby was a small mountain.

At last a wise old woman pointed her cane to the top of the mountain.

At the top of the mount was the kiva of an old burrowing owl and his wife.

"There! Hear what Grandfather Burrowing Owl has to say."

They chose a young prairie dog to talk to the burrowing owl.

Tap . . . tap . . . tap, poured the rain.

The prairie dog climbed to the top of
the mountain.
He stopped on the roof of the kiva.

He stood on his hind legs and cried,
"Wek wek, wek wek!"

The burrowing owl stepped out.
He was not in a very good mood.

He said, "Whoo-whoo-o-o's there?
It is not the way of your people to come
to my kiva and make such noise."
He blinked his big brown eyes.

The prairie dog shook hands with the
burrowing owl.

"What do you want?" asked the owl.
"I heard you chattering down below."

"Grandfather," said the prairie dog,
"my people are very hungry.
Our meadows have been flooded by
the Rain Gods.
We need your help.
Pretty soon we will all drown."

"Whoo . . . whum, indeed," said the owl.
He scratched his chin with his claw.

"Go back to your people.
I will think of a way.
I will have an answer in four days."

The prairie dog said farewell.
He climbed down to his village below.

Next day the owl asked his wife,
"Put on a large pot of beans.
Use the kind that smells bad."

The burrowing owl hunted around
the roots of bushes.
At last he found a smelly tip beetle.
He snatched him up in his claws.

"My friend," said the burrowing owl,
"I do not wish to hurt you.
You are welcome in my house.
Eat all the beans you want."

"Good friend," said the tip beetle.
He sat down at the bowl of beans.
He ate and swallowed and gulped.

He ate three bowls of beans.
"Thank you," he burped.
"I A-AM FULL."

The owl took a buckskin pouch.
"Please blow up this pouch," he said.

He thanked the tip beetle for his help.

Outside the rain was rattling, rattling.

On the fourth day, the owl took the bag
of bad smell out to his rooftop.

He took up a stick and hit it.
Once – whack! Twice – whack!
He gave it a final hit – whack!

Behold! The clouds puffed away
to a far off mountaintop.
The Rain Gods couldn't stand the smell.

"Wek wek, wek wek, wek wek!"
The prairie dogs were very happy.
They cheered a good dry day to
Grandfather Burrowing Owl.

And for that reason prairie dogs and
burrowing owls have always been
good friends.

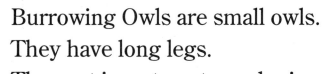

Burrowing Owls are small owls.
They have long legs.
They eat insects, rats, and mice.
Sometimes they eat cactus fruit.

Burrowing Owls live in old
prairie dog holes.
They make a sound like a rattlesnake.
This scares others away from
their holes.

The Hopi name for Burrowing Owl is
*Ko'ko*, "watcher of the dark."

America's tiniest
owl is the Elf Owl.
It is only about
six inches tall.
It eats many kinds
of insects.

Owls can't move their eyes.
They turn their heads instead.

Screech Owl

# STOLEN BABY

A Picuris Story

"A-weh, a-weh," cried a Picuris baby.
It cried day and night.

The baby cried all the time.
The mother did not know what to do.

She sang soft cradle songs.

Still the baby cried, "A-weh, a-weh."

The next night the mother took the
baby out on the roof.
She left it all alone.

An owl flew by and heard the baby cry.

"Who-oo's baby is crying?
That baby will be mine."

Then the owl flew to the roof.
She picked up the baby in her claws.
She blinked her big eyes with joy.

The owl carried the baby to her nest
on a mountaintop.

Each day the owl would feed the baby
what she could.

The baby stayed cradled in the nest.

One night, a hunter passed by.
He heard the baby cry, "A-weh, a-weh."
He put a hand to his ear and listened.

"A-weh, a-weh," cried the baby.

"That sounds like a baby crying,"
said the hunter.
He climbed to the top of the rocks.

There at the top sat the baby crying.

"Little one, we will find your mother."
He took the baby in his arms.
He sang to it as he rode.
He carried it to the village.

The hunter walked into the village.
He took the baby to its mother's kiva.

He knocked once . . . twice . . .
Knock knock!

The mother opened the door slowly.

"Why did you leave your baby outside?"

"I didn't know what else to do,"
said the mother.

The hunter said, "I found your baby at
the home of an owl."

He handed the baby to its mother.
The mother was happy to see her baby.

"If it were not for me, the owl could
have eaten your baby!"

The mother said, "I will not leave my
baby to cry outside alone.
The owl will not take my baby again."

She thanked the hunter.
And since then no Picuris mother has
ever left her baby outside alone.

The baby grew up strong.
Whenever he saw an owl
he remembered and smiled.

Young Barn Owl–three weeks old

Male and female owls look the same.
Females are bigger than males.

Baby owls are called owlets.
They have soft feathers called down.
Parents feed the babies until they can
fly and hunt alone.

An owl feather
is put next to
a Zuni baby
to help it sleep.

Owl claws are large and sharp.
They are called talons.

Owls help keep our land free of
rats and mice.
It is against the law in the United
States to hurt or kill any owl.

Zuni Pottery Owl

# GLOSSARY

**Buckskin:** Soft leather made from deerskin

**Cardinal:** A red bird common to eastern North America

**Cherokee** (chair´-o-kee): An Indian nation of southeastern North America

**Eskimo** (es´-ki-moe): A native people of the far north

**Heron** (hair´-un): A large North American wading bird

**Hopi** (hoe´-pee): An Indian nation of the desert Southwest

**Kiva** (kee´-vah): A Pueblo pit house; now used for religious rites

**Panther:** A big cat of eastern North America; like a cougar

**Picuris** (pick´-a-ris): A Pueblo nation of the desert Southwest

**Salish** (say´-lish): An Indian nation of the Pacific Northwest

**Seneca** (sen´-a-ca): One of the six Iroquois nations of the Eastern Woodlands

**Tip Beetle:** A kind of beetle that smells bad

**Zuni** (zoo´-nee): A Pueblo nation of the desert Southwest